Hebron Public Library
201 W. Sigler Street
Hebron, IN 46341

PAUL MEETS BERNADETTE

ROSY LAMB

PORTER COUNTY PUBLIC LIBRARY

Hebron Public Library
201 W. Sigler Street
Hebron, IN 46341

CANDLEWICK PRESS

JJ FIC HEB
LAMB
DISCARD
Lamb, Rosy, author, illustrato
Paul meets Bernadette /
33410012644318 12/16/13

Paul used to go around in circles.

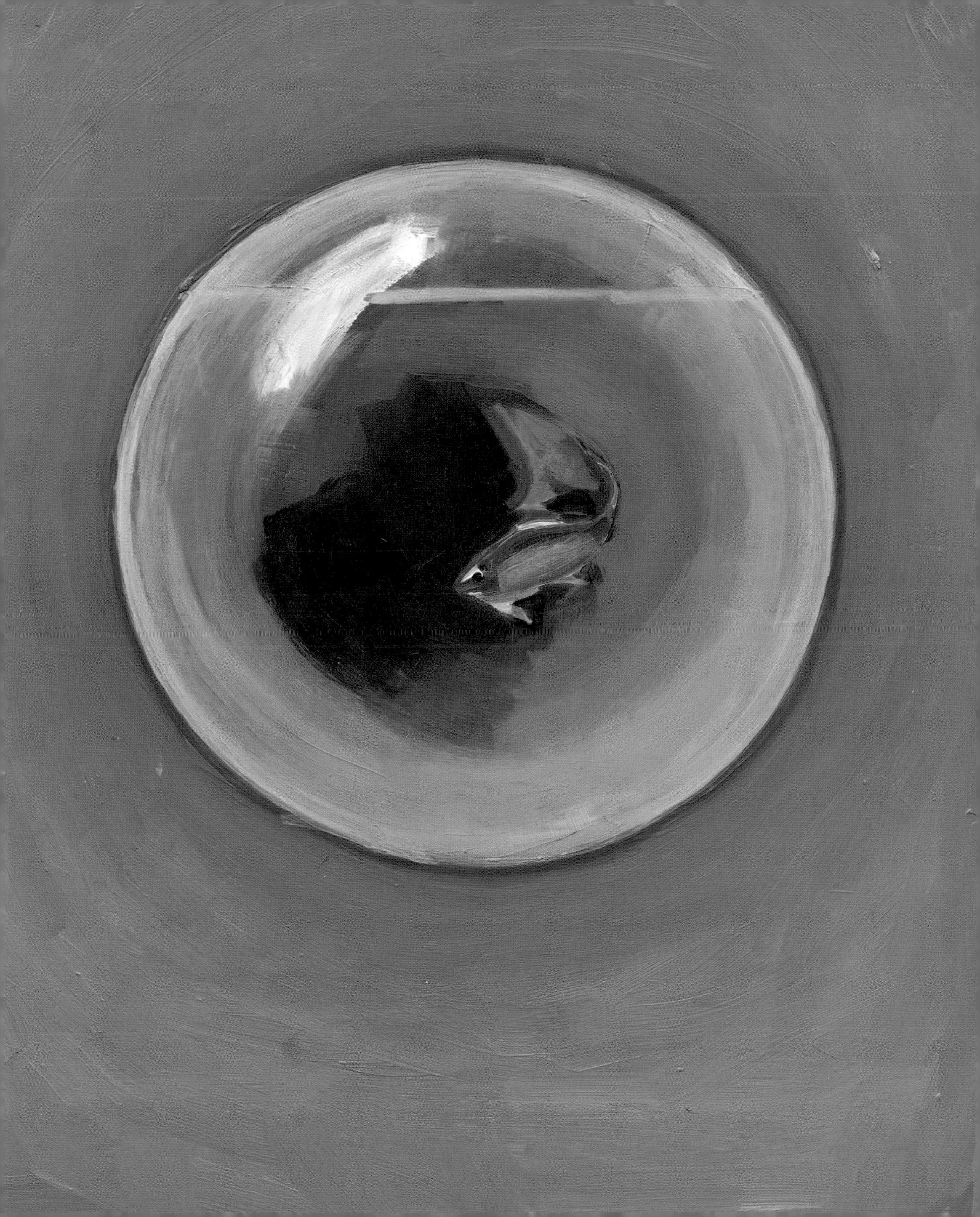

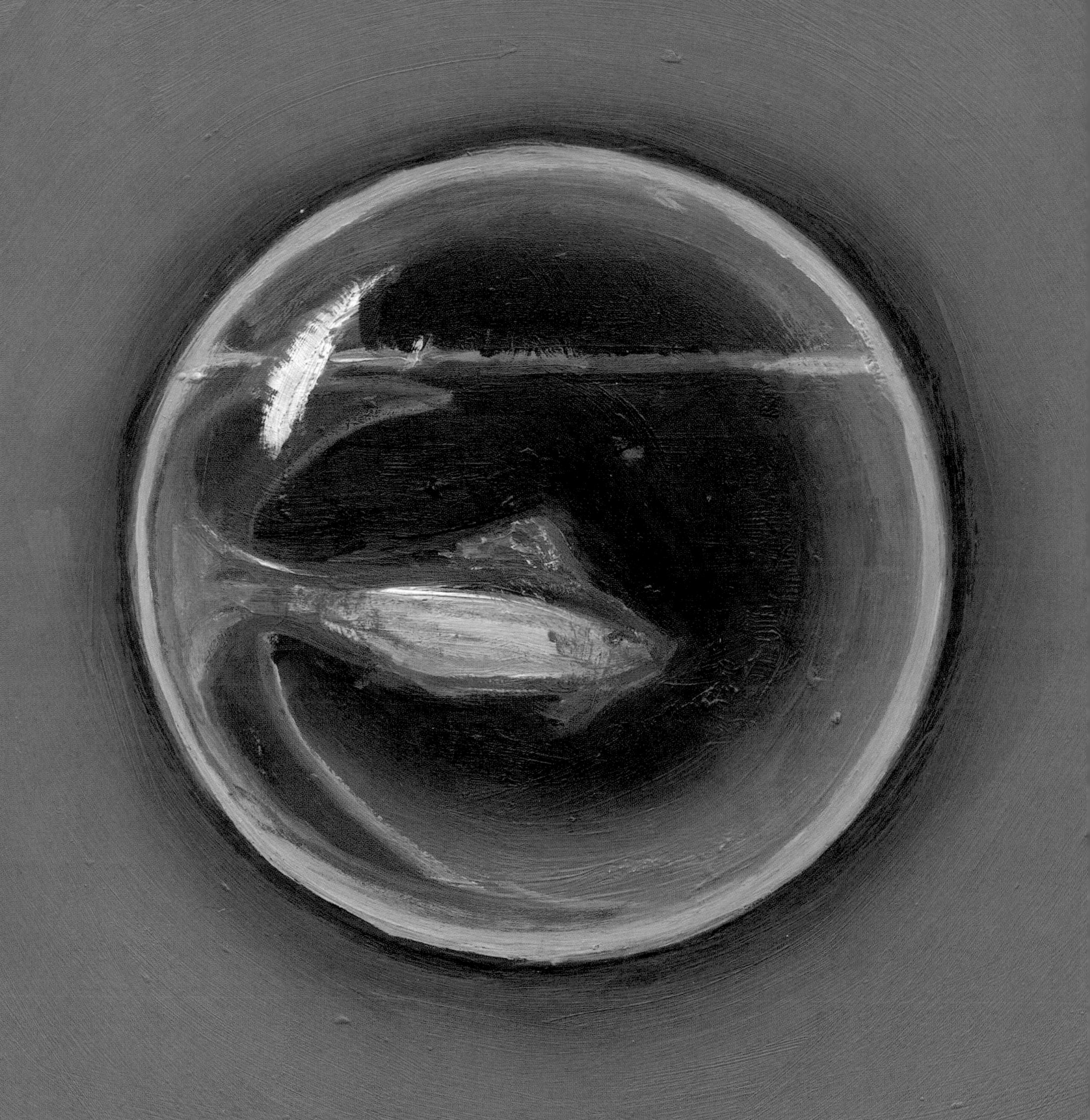

He made big circles

and little circles.

He circled from left to right

and from right to left.

He circled from top to bottom

and from bottom to top.

And then one day, Bernadette dropped in.

"What are you doing?" Bernadette asks Paul.

"I'm going round and round," says Paul. "What else is there to do?"

"Haven't you ever noticed that there's a whole world out there? There are so many things to see. Come look over here."

“What do you think that yellow thing is?” asks Bernadette.

“Hum de dum . . .” says Paul.

“That,” says Bernadette, “is a boat!”

“Paul, come over here,” says Bernadette.
“Do you see the forest with trees of every color?”
“Yes, I do,” says Paul. “How enchanting!’

“Do you see that round thing off in the distance? What do you think that is?” asks Bernadette.

“I just can’t think,” answers Paul.

“That,” says Bernadette, “is a cactus!”

XII
I
II
III
IV
V
VI
VII
VIII
IX
X
XI

“Aha,” says Paul. “And what is that draped up there?”

“Why, that is a lady’s dress!”

“Oh, that is a dress! Of course, of course. What else could it be?” Paul says. “And I think it would look very pretty on you.”

Paul spots something big and blue. "What is that?" he asks Bernadette.

"That," says Bernadette, "is an elephant."

“Is she a dangerous elephant?” asks Paul.

“She is not *too* dangerous,” Bernadette tells Paul. “But you must not disturb her when she is feeding her babies.”

"Look up, over there!" Bernadette exclaims. "A lunetta butterfly!"

How lovely she is, thinks Paul.

"And do you see the tall buildings over there?" says Bernadette. "That is a city."

"What is the name of the city?" asks Paul.

"Milkwaukee," Bernadette tells him.

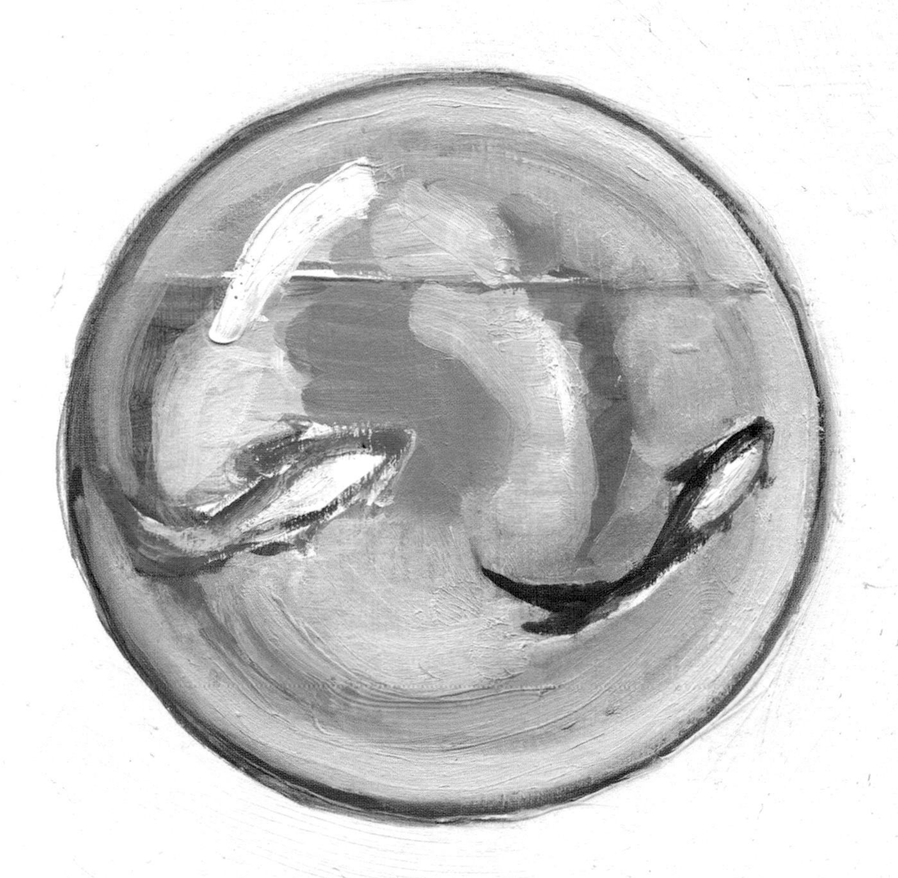

OPEN →
MILK
NATURALLY
ORANGE JUICE
FROM THE ISLE OF
Concentrate
DAIRY MAID
MILK

"Are those two bright-yellow circles down there fried eggs?" Paul asks Bernadette.

"Are you crazy?" says Bernadette. "Of course they are not fried eggs! That is the sun and the moon!"

AND YOU, BERNADETTE, ARE MY STAR

“There is just one more thing in the whole world,” says Bernadette.

“What is it?” asks Paul.

Bernadette motions down below and tells him, “It’s a . . .”

“fish!”

Bernadette has shown Paul the whole world, and so Paul doesn't go around in circles anymore. He has something so much better to do.

Now Paul goes around Bernadette.

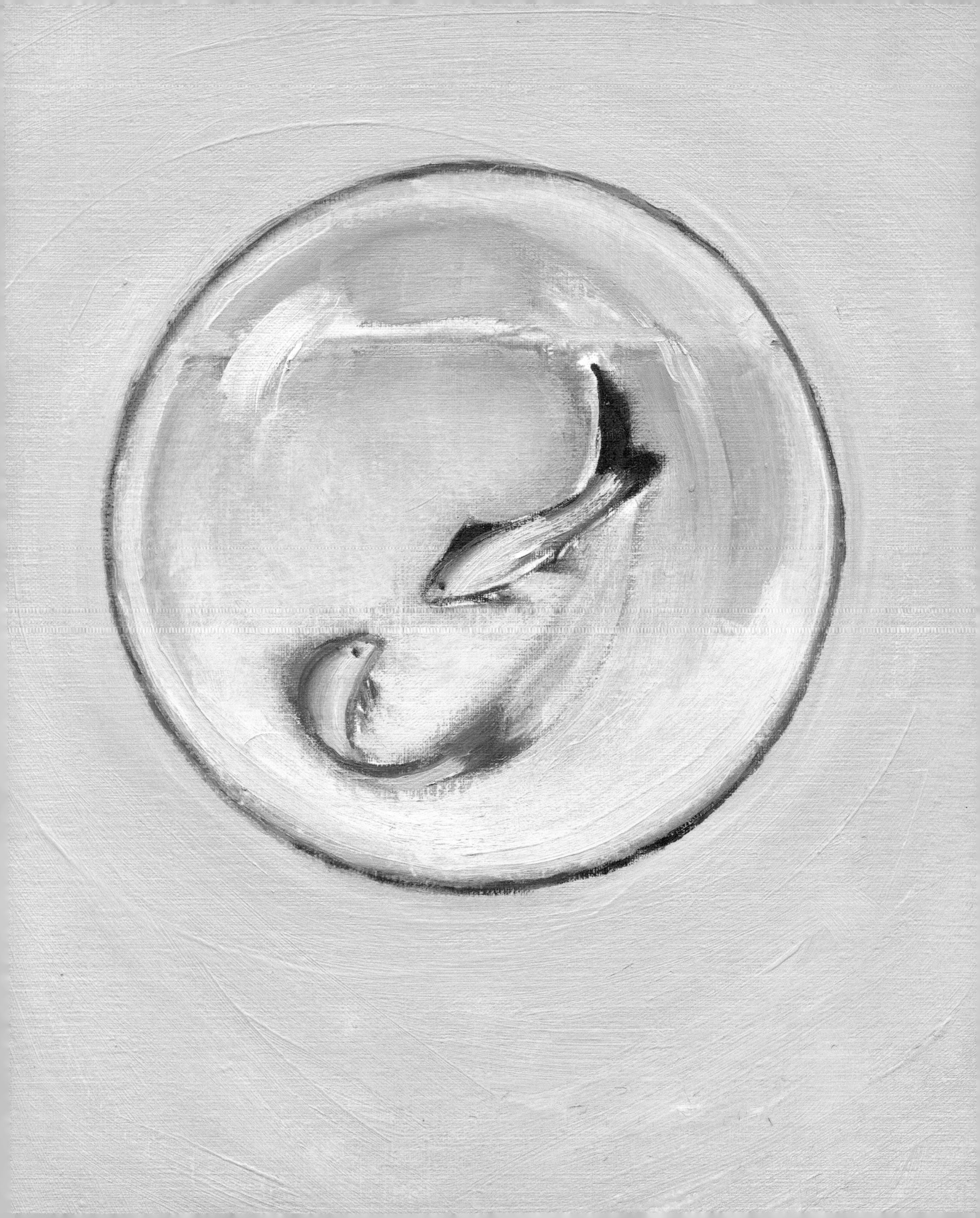

For Meena, my little fish

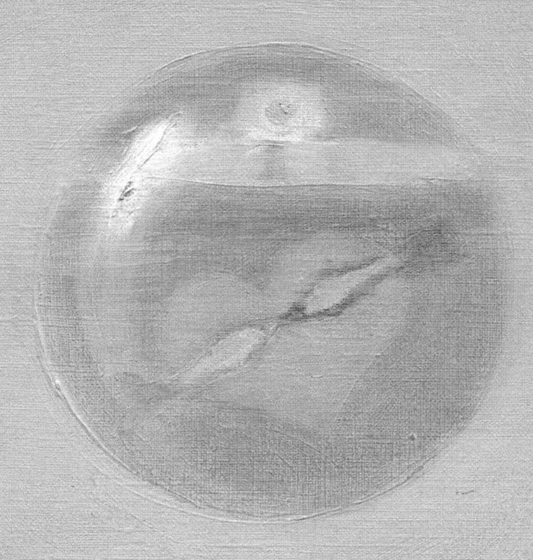

Thanks to the art director, Maryellen Hanley, whose clarity of vision shows at every turn of the page, and to my husband, Karthik, for helping me dust off the little book I mocked up years ago.

Copyright © 2013 by Rosy Lamb

All rights reserved. No part of this book may be reproduced, transmitted, or stored in an information retrieval system in any form or by any means, graphic, electronic, or mechanical, including photocopying, taping, and recording, without prior written permission from the publisher.

First edition 2013

Library of Congress Catalog Card Number 2012947712
ISBN 978-0-7636-6130-4

13 14 15 16 17 18 TLF 10 9 8 7 6 5 4 3 2 1

Printed in Dongguan, Guangdong, China

This book was typeset in Hightower.
The illustrations were done in oil.

Candlewick Press
99 Dover Street
Somerville, Massachusetts 02144

visit us at www.candlewick.com